NO LONGER PROPERTY OF THE SEATTLE PUBLIC LIBRARY

Treasure Trap

Owlkids Books

Chirp, Tweet, and Squawk loved to play in their playhouse. On this particular day, they were playing…

"Treasure hunters!" suggested Tweet.

"Treasure hunters in the jungle!" added Squawk.

"Treasure hunters in the jungle, where they find a pyramid made of gold!" continued Chirp.

"Maybe there's gold *inside* the pyramid, too!" said Treasure Hunter Squawk. "Let's go!"

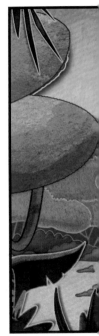

"Wait! We need to be careful," said Treasure Hunter Chirp.

"Yeah, I have a funny feeling about this place," said Treasure Hunter Tweet.

"You guys worry too much," said Treasure Hunter Squawk, hurrying up the stairs of the pyramid. "What could possibly go wrong?"

Inside the golden pyramid, the three treasure hunters found...

"More gold!" yelled Squawk.

"So much gold! So shiny..." said Tweet.

"Be careful what you touch," said Chirp. "There could be traps!"

"What could possibly go wrong if I just touch this crown...or this necklace...or this statue?" asked Squawk.

Suddenly, the floor opened up beneath their feet...

"I set off a trap!" said Squawk. "How do we get out of this pit?"

"Hang on, Squawk!" said Tweet. "We'll use you as a ladder to climb out."

"We've got to get out of this pyramid!" said Chirp.

"We've got to get some treasure first!" said Squawk. "Like this golden popcorn!"

"Don't touch the popcorn, Squawk! You'll set off another trap!" said Chirp.

"The walls are closing in on us!" said Tweet.

"Look inside the treasure chest for something to help us out," said Chirp.

"But you said not to touch anything!" said Squawk.

"He means look in the box—I mean, the treasure chest—with all the helpful stuff," said Tweet.

The three friends opened the lid and looked inside.

"Are you sure there are no traps in there?" asked Squawk.

"No traps but lots of comic books, broken crayons, tin foil…" said Tweet.

"And wedges!" said Chirp.

"Wedges?" asked Squawk.

"Big wedges are like ramps," said Chirp, "and smaller wedges can be used to hold doors open…and that gives me an idea!"

Back inside the golden pyramid, the walls were closing in on treasure hunters Chirp, Tweet, and Squawk...

"Hurry up! I don't want to get squashed!" yelled Tweet.

"You won't! Jam these wedges underneath the walls," said Chirp.

"It's working!" said Squawk. "The wedges are keeping the walls from closing!"

"Look here," said Tweet. "There's a secret passageway!"

"That's our way out," said Chirp. "Just don't touch anything, Squawk!"

"I'm not touching anything," said Squawk. "I'm just resting against this wall."

But leaning against the wall set off the worst trap yet...

"Where did that giant rock come from?" asked Squawk.

"It's another trap!" said Tweet. "Run!"

"We can't outrun that thing!" said Chirp. "We need to find a way to stop it!"

"Can we use the wedges?" asked Tweet.

"Yes!" said Chirp. "We can use them to make a ramp!"

Treasure hunters Chirp, Tweet, and Squawk used the small wedges to build a big ramp.

"Duck, you guys!" yelled Squawk, as the giant rock rolled up the ramp and over their heads.

"Look!" said Tweet. "The rock made a not-so-secret passageway!"

"And now we have a way out of here!" said Chirp.

"Way to escape those traps, treasure hunters!" said Chirp.

"Too bad we didn't get any treasure," said Tweet.

"Speak for yourself!" said Squawk. "Behold...the golden popcorn!"

From an episode of the animated TV series *Chirp*, produced by Sinking Ship (Chirp) Productions. Based on the Chirp character created by Bob Kain.

Based on the TV episode *Treasure Trap* written by Brendan Russell. Story adaptation written by J. Torres.

CHIRP and the CHIRP character are trademarks of Bayard Presse Canada Inc.

Text © 2016 Owlkids Books Inc.
Interior illustrations by Smiley Guy Studios. © 2016 Sinking Ship (Chirp) Productions. Used under license.
Cover illustration by Cale Atkinson, based on images from the TV episode. Cover illustration © 2016 Owlkids Books Inc.

All rights reserved. No part of this publication may be reproduced, stored in a retrieval system, or transmitted in any form or by any means, without the prior written permission of Owlkids Books Inc., or in the case of photocopying or other reprographic copying, a license from the Canadian Copyright Licensing Agency (Access Copyright). For an Access Copyright license, visit www.accesscopyright.ca or call toll-free to 1-800-893-5777.

Owlkids Books acknowledges the financial support of the Canada Council for the Arts, the Ontario Arts Council, the Government of Canada through the Canada Book Fund (CBF) and the Government of Ontario through the Ontario Media Development Corporation's Book Initiative for our publishing activities.

Published in Canada by
Owlkids Books Inc.
10 Lower Spadina Avenue
Toronto, ON M5V 2Z2

Cataloguing data available from Library and Archives Canada.

ISBN 978-1-77147-187-9

Edited by: Jennifer Stokes
Designed by: Susan Sinclair

Canadä

ONTARIO ARTS COUNCIL
CONSEIL DES ARTS DE L'ONTARIO
an Ontario government agency
un organisme du gouvernement de l'Ontario

Canada Council for the Arts   Conseil des Arts du Canada

Manufactured in Shenzhen, China, in September 2015, by C&C Joint Printing Co.
Job #HP4362

A   B   C   D   E   F

 Publisher of Chirp, chickaDEE and OWL
www.owlkidsbooks.com

Owlkids Books is a division of